To Daisy, the newest member of our family, who was rescued from the local tip.
– Colin

In memory of Pickles, my first doggy friend.
– Sarah

Written by
Colin Thompson

Illustrated by
Sarah Davis

ABC
Books

When a new baby is born it's difficult to tell if it will grow up to be

Big

Or small

or **BRAVE**

or scared of the dark and spiders.

So sometimes, babies get the wrong name.

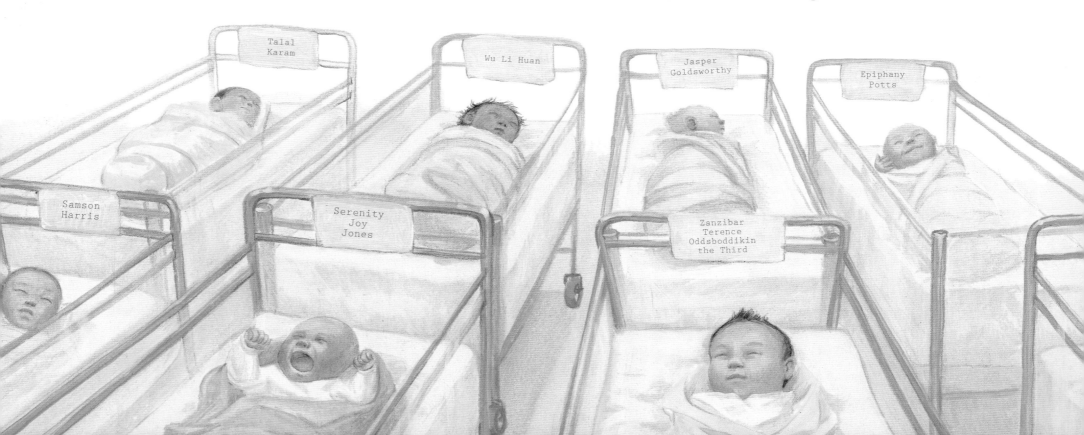

There are lots of people
called Bruce
who should probably
be called Julian.

There are even some people
called Bruce who should be
called Beryl, and others
who should be called Fido.

It's the same with dogs.

So when the Claybourne-Willments,
who should have been called
the Smiths, got Fearless
as a little puppy

it seemed a good name for him.

Except Fearless wasn't.

If a car backfired in the street,
so did Fearless.

House-training was hard
for Fearless.

Bulldogs have big heads,
but most of it is
very thick bone.

They can run into walls
and hardly notice,
but inside the thick bone
there isn't much room
for a brain.

So Fearless had a terrible time understanding why it was
all right to go on the grass which his dad spent hours mowing
and not on the carpet which his dad took no notice of at all.

He was very careful never to go on the newspapers his mum left
lying on the kitchen floor at night, in case she wanted to read them.

He might have had a tiny
nervous brain, but he had
a huge heart and loved everyone.

He even loved the vet
who stuck needles in him.

He loved the vet so much
he once licked her contact lens out.

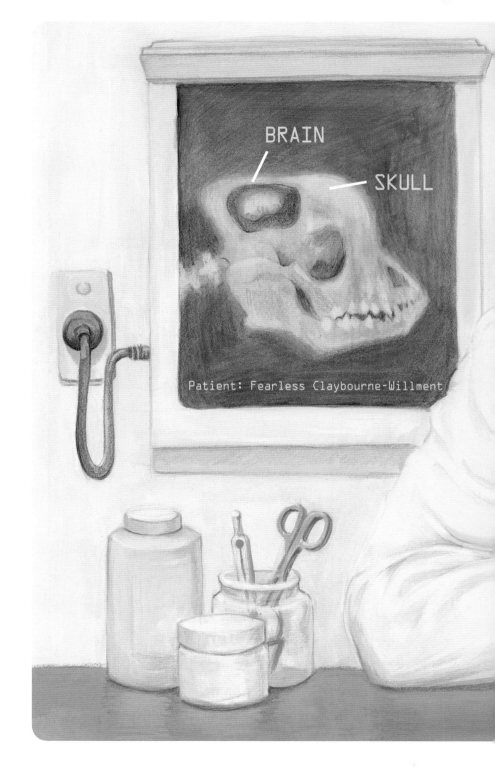

BRAIN

SKULL

Patient: Fearless Claybourne-Willment

After that, the vet always wore glasses
when Fearless went to see her.

Best of all Fearless loved children,
especially the small one that
crawled around on the floor.

She loved Fearless too because
when she tried to give her dolls
a biscuit, nothing happened,

but when she gave one to Fearless
he looked very happy
and ate it.

Fearless knew that it was his job
to protect his family from
all the frightening things in the world
and be brave – even when he wasn't.

There were scary things everywhere.

Whenever Mrs Jones
came to the house,
a dangerous black handbag
used to follow her and sit
on the floor by her chair.

Fearless would back away growling
until his mum trapped the handbag
under a cushion.

He had to keep his eye on the broom too, because once when he went into the laundry, it fell on him and tried to bite him.

And as for the stairs, he just didn't want to think about them. He'd tried to climb them when he had been a puppy and they had tripped him up

and made him fall down on his head.

Fearless was as soft as custard and wouldn't hurt a fly,
except when he sat on one once and squashed it.

But people who didn't know him used to cross the road because they thought he wanted to bite them, when he was really just smiling hello.

And then one night Fearless lived up to his name.

Everyone had gone to bed and
forgotten to lock the back door.

Fearless was lying in his bed by the fridge, watching the moonlight crawl across
his dinner bowl, when someone opened the door and came into the house.

It wasn't one of his friends.

It was a man in
a funny hat that
covered half his face.

Fearless stood up and wagged his tail as the man picked up his mum's handbag.

'Hello,' Fearless said in his friendliest voice.

The man stopped.

He looked at Fearless,
said a rude word
and jumped on to the table.

**'You're not supposed to
put your feet on the table,'**
said Fearless, but the man
just heard big dog barks
and looked scared.

Fearless's dad heard the big barks too and came downstairs.

'**Look, look,** Dad,
that **naughty** man's got
his feet on the table,'

Fearless shouted and he tried to

jump up and pull the man's shoelaces.

The man leapt in the air,
dropped the handbag
and ran out of the door.

'Rude man,' said Fearless to himself. 'He didn't even say goodbye.'

'Who's a big brave fearless dog then?'
said his dad as he patted Fearless
on the head and gave him a
piece of cheese.

'Is that a trick question?'
thought Fearless as he
went back to sleep.

The next day his mum bought him a **huge** bone ...

... which looked so **frightening,**
Fearless had to bury it in the garden.

The 'ABC Wave' device and the 'ABC KIDS'
device are trademarks of the Australian
Broadcasting Corporation and are used under
licence by HarperCollins*Publishers* Australia.

First published in Australia in 2009
This edition published in 2014
by HarperCollins*Children'sBooks*
a division of HarperCollins*Publishers* Australia Pty Limited
ABN 36 009 913 517
harpercollins.com.au

Copyright text © Colin Thompson 2009
Copyright illustrations © Sarah Davis 2009

The rights of Colin Thompson and Sarah Davis to be identified as the
author and illustrator of this work have been asserted by them in
accordance with the *Copyright Amendment (Moral Rights) Act 2000*.

HarperCollins*Publishers*
Level 13, 201 Elizabeth Street, Sydney, NSW 2000, Australia
Unit D1, 63 Apollo Drive, Rosedale, Auckland 0632, New Zealand

A CiP record is available from the National Library of Australia.
ISBN: 978 0 7333 3082 7

Designed by Sarah Davis; Typeset in Hunniwell by Sarah Davis
Colour reproduction by Graphic Print Group, Adelaide
Printed in China by RR Donnelley on 128 gsm Matt Art

17 16 15 14   15 16 17 18